The Big House

Alice's Dream

Alice's Dream
Meggi Bamford

First impression 1986
by J. M. Pearson & Son (Publishers) Ltd.,
The Midland Railway Grain Warehouse,
Burton-on-Trent, Staffordshire.

Typeset by Characters of Taunton, Somerset.
Printed by Penwell of Callington, Cornwall.

British Library Cataloguing in Publication Data

Bamford, Meggi
   Alice's Dream.
I. Title
823'.914(J) PZ7

ISBN 0 907864 40 6

Introduction

This book illustrates the contents of an attic, which is in fact now a private museum. Everything has been collected over the years, and restored: the pictures in the dolls houses are made from Victorian buttons, the tiny little paintings on the walls are hand done; whilst the furnishings are all authentic and have been painstakingly collected from all over England.

If one is feeling a little lonely, one's thoughts often revert to childhood days, when a well-worn doll or a grubby bunny-rabbit was of great comfort. These loved toys knew all the baby secrets of their former owners.

One day, when casually walking along a street in Kensington, I suddenly stopped by a shop window and saw a pathetic little doll looking neglected, dressed in raggy clothes. Up until that moment I had no interest in dolls or toys. The price was Two pounds Two shillings and Sixpence.

My feelings of sympathy induced me to buy this doll along with a little horse on wheels.

The doll sat on a chair in my drawing room for several months. One day a little girl came with her mother. Her first remark was "What a poor little doll, her clothes are so very worn and so old, she should be smart like my doll". She took her own little doll and compared the two.

She apparently thought it was my doll from childhood. Her next remark was,"If that was your doll when you were a little girl, you must be very, very old, because dolls are made like mine today", meaning her doll was made of plastic, and the other had a china head! Then she added,"When I am an old, old lady I will still have my doll, because I am always going to have her with me".

When tea was over and the little girl and her mother had gone, I looked at the doll and had to agree with my little friend. Why should old dolls and toys always end up looking shabby, grubby and forlorn?

This was the beginning of the adventure of collecting. I found an old petticoat with beautiful layers of lace, belonging to my Grandmother and a piece of fine cream flannel, also very old. From these I made under-clothes and a dress. From a pair of Victorian white kid-gloves, badly worn at the fingers, I endeavoured to make the shoes, using the tiny pearl buttons to fasten the straps. The results fascinated me, they looked exactly like the original clothes would have in the year 1890 and, of course, the materials were the right age. In a few weeks the doll was transformed from the poor little urchin into a Society Lady ready for a glorious sunny day at Ascot!

I was thrilled with my new pastime and felt a deep sense of satisfaction. It was extremely difficult at times when I found my fingers were too big to sew the little sleeves in the dress, and almost impossible to find a sewing needle small enough to go through the tiny holes in the buttons, press studs and hooks and eyes, which I may add were minute and very old. I was determined not to use the sewing machine and to do everything by hand, as in days gone by.

As the years passed, my collecting continued, and I now have so many dolls, each one painstakingly dressed with clothes made from Victorian and pre-Victorian dresses given to me by kind friends who have discovered them in cobwebby trunks in their dusty attics. Also I have frequently visited the well known sales-rooms in London, looking for lace, baby robes and the necessary items to use. It almost became an obsession. Apart from the collecting, it was of tremendous interest to meet other people from different parts of the world, who have the same hobbies. The Antique dealers are also very friendly people, they come to you and ask if you have a 'Bru' doll in your collection, or would you like to include a 'Jumeau' doll along with the other ones that you have.

'The Collection in the Attic' featured herein, has been put together with great love and devotion for the sake of antiquity, as a memorial to past ages, and for the love that the toys have had in days gone by from the children to whom they have belonged.

A good deal of research has gone into the authenticity of each article. I have endeavoured to make "Alice's Dream" both informative and entertaining, and as correct as it possibly can be for fellow collectors. The accompanying 'stories' were written for children of all ages who, I hope, might be encouraged to preserve for themselves their own precious things of the past.

Meggi Bamford

Acknowledgements

The author extends grateful thanks to: Michael Lee and John Clayton for their photographs and illustrations respectively; Anthony Bamford for loan of photographic equipment; Kenneth Bradley, curator for the toys in The Attic; Hazel Norman for her typing work; Thomas Gaunt; David Cowen; Jackie Stewart; Mary Kendall; and Mark Bamford.

The publishers are indebted to the three 'Js' - Janet Hoult, who designed the book; Joy Hales who edited it; and Joan Plachta who publicised it. Additional thanks are due to Don Hume, who made the initial connection; John Masters for injections of enthusiasm at just the right intervals; Lynne Howard and her delightful daughters Elizabeth and Lucy; Mark Curnock and staff of Characters who typeset the text almost on the move; and to Adrian High, Tom Warren and staff of Penwell who turned the 'dream' into reality!

Please Look...

High up in the big house where my Grandma lives are lots of rooms. The room we like best of all she calls 'The Attic'.

The attic is full of tiny treasures far too precious for a little girl like me to play with. Sometimes my little brother and I are allowed to peep through the window. I would love to play with all the toys. Grandma tells me that they are very old and so fragile, but one day when I am older, I may possess them. I know I will take great care of them. Would you like to share the attic with me?

Tomorrow I will tell you all about it, because it is my bedtime now. Nanny has brought the supper into the nursery, after that I will feel very sleepy and far too tired to talk.

My name is Alice. My little brother is Joseph. He doesn't understand about the toys in the attic. I try to explain, but all he can do is laugh and laugh.

With love

From Alice

Alice and her little brother are well and truly tucked up in bed, and away Alice goes into dreamland.

By this time all the household are fast asleep. Now is the time for all the little people in the attic to come alive.

Alice dreams on. There are so many little stories that come into her dreams, going back for generations. Very, very happy memories for most of the occupants of the attic and a few sad ones. For instance there is Amelia, who is almost 150 years old. She is very stern, so well-disciplined. She imagines she is the head over everyone - she is highly respected.

Her face is made of wax. 70 years ago, she belonged to a little girl who loved her very much. Unfortunately, this little girl held Amelia by the fire in the Drawing Room. Consequently, after a short time the heat from the fire melted Amelia's nose. She was carefully restored with a new nose. After this incident she was taken great care of and here she is to this day, feeling very fortunate to be in the attic. Not very pretty, but all her friends are so kind to her, and they do like her.

You will meet Amelia and all her friends in the following pages of this book.

To my dear grandchildren:

Alice Camille, Joseph Cyril, and George Harry Anthony

Chapter

1

Leaving the
Attic

Martha & Mildred

Martha and I have been invited to Aunt Sophia's house for tea. It is a great occasion. She is very kind, she enjoys having friends and relations calling to see her. We look forward to her delicious cakes. Although Martha is not the least bit thrilled with the seed cake Aunt Sophia presents us with (Martha detests caraway seeds), out of sheer politeness and because she adores Aunt Sophia, she eats the cake. Aunt Sophia also serves hot muffins in a superb silver muffin dish. We both love these. The cucumber sandwiches are also very tasty.

Aunt Sophia lived in America for many years, that is why she makes her muffins the American way. She puts blueberries, cinnamon or even cranberries in them. She has also lived in England, so likes to serve her muffins for afternoon tea. It is quite the opposite in America where muffins are served at the breakfast table. I suppose, after all, that afternoon tea is only an English custom.

"Oh Mildred! Are you completely ready? It is almost three o'clock. We have a very long way to walk."

"Thank goodness, it isn't raining today" murmurs Mildred.

Amelia & Anna

Amelia and Anna have lived in the attic for many years. Before that, Amelia belonged to a little girl in the year 1860. Her face is made of wax. Unfortunately, one Sunday afternoon, her little owner – who incidentally was only allowed to play with her on Sundays – held her by the fire in the Drawing Room. It was sad, her face began to melt with the heat, her little nose just vanished. Anyhow, it wasn't beyond repair. Soon she had a new nose. Living here she finds that the atmosphere is just right – not too hot – so there is no chance of the same accident happening again.

Both Amelia and Anna enjoy looking after the babies. They take full charge. Tonight it is Adam they are taking care of. Adam has three faces. He is unusual. One face cries, turn his head around and another face laughs, turn his head around again and then he is sleeping. He never cries – he is always laughing or sleeping.

He thinks his tiny bed is very smart. Before it found its way into the attic, a lady was using it to put flowers in. Can you imagine! Flowers in Adam's cot. He would not like it if he knew.

Josephine & Joanna

We are Josephine and Joanna. We were both born in the year of 1860, and are the same age as Amelia and Anna. Our faces are also made of wax. We appreciate living in the attic. There is not the slightest chance of our wax faces melting, it is so cool.

Both our dresses are original. Joanna's dress is really beautiful. It has lace epaulettes that should hang from her shoulders over her arms, but she prefers to pull it high to her neck. It has a magnificent full skirt with fine hemstitching around the bottom.

My dress is fine lawn material with broderie Anglaise lace round the edge. I am wearing a sweet little lace bonnet.

We are going to a party with Lucinda. Our hairdresser has taken great care not to comb out too much hair. Being so old, we can lose our hair very quickly. If this happens we will not retain our value or attraction.

Priscilla

My name is Priscilla. I have decided not to go to a party tonight, simply because my party dress has somehow been mislaid. That is not the least bit surprising since it was made in the year 1875. The dress I am wearing now was also made at the same time.

It is so interesting to watch my friends preparing to go out. Their discussions are very amusing as to what they are going to wear, or what they are going to do.

I do not really mind remaining in the attic. Amelia and Anna will be here and I have a very interesting book to read called "Little Snow Shoes". It has beautiful pictures and lovely poems in it.

Grandma

Grandma adores her old bed. It is made of mahogany wood. It is called a half tester. It was made in the early 19th century and has beautiful tapestry drapes and a velvet back the same age as the bed.

Grandma must have been a lady of society because she has a crest and a crown embroidered on the pillow case, sheets and blankets. The pillow case is silk.

In her bureau at the side of her bed, she keeps important papers, but in the top she has tiny, tiny little bottles of various designs; an unusual collection.

Why Grandma is still in bed is quite a question, because everyone is going to have great fun. We all know she loves her old bed – perhaps she thinks someone may steal it if she leaves it.

There are so many little people in the attic, they look so beautiful in their magnificent dresses. Everyone is dancing, singing and playing. Who knows, Grandma may change her mind.

Lucy, Lindy & Lucinda

Three Grand-daughters, Lucy, Lindy and Lucinda, try to persuade Grandma to join them in the activities of the attic, but to no avail. Her reply is, "No thank you my dears, it is getting late. You run along, and I will look forward to your return. I will be delighted to hear all the news of your adventures."

Lucinda, who admires all Grandma's beautiful antique furniture, is always fascinated with the Cheval mirror. She is looking at herself and imagines she will be going to the Ball with her handsome Prince.

Karolina

Karolina is beautiful in every way. She is genteel and very thoughtful. She came from Paris. Her dress was made in France. Her elegant lace hat completes the outfit. The dress is made of very fine muslin, with insertions of delicate 19th century Alençon lace. It has blue ribbon threaded through, with blue ribbon bows hanging down the back.

At the moment she is in charge of Jemima, but after a while Priscilla says she will take care of Jemima. Karolina will then go with her friends to see the gardens.

Priscilla likes reading her books when she is left in charge of the babies.

Caron, Catherine & Coral

We are Caron, Catherine and Coral. This afternoon we are going out for a treat. Mummie has been so busy washing and starching our dresses. She says it is a very tedious occupation because the dresses must be ironed whilst they are still wet. They also have to be ironed on the wrong side to enable the embroidery to stand out and look so beautiful.

How lovely! We are going to see Alice's ponies. One is called Twiggy – she is very small and her coat is brown. I think Twiggy is a little Welsh pony. Another pony is called Joey. He is always getting into mischief. He loves to prance around in the rain. When it is snowing he runs and canters around the field. He is a very funny pony. He is black and has a long tail and a thick shiny mane.

Mummie says we may help Alice to feed the horses with hay and oats. We cannot help to groom them. This is rather a dusty job. It would be dreadful if we were to get our dresses dirty. Mummie would never forgive us.

After spending one hour with the ponies and horses, and really enjoying every minute, Alice's Mummie brought the loveliest tea for us to eat. Much nicer than an ordinary picnic. We had fruit, jellies and the most scrumptious chocolate cake. Mmm, it was delicious.

Catherine and Coral are so tired, they would like to return to the attic, but I am so wide awake I would like this dream to go on for ever and ever.

Angela

Catherine asked me to go with her and Caron and Coral but I don't feel very well today; though I may perhaps go out with Nanny after I have had a rest.

The thing is, I have hurt my little finger – can you see? The Nursery floor is highly polished, it looks beautiful and very shiny, but I slipped and fell down with a big bump. I do not know why grown-ups expect dolls like me to walk straight! I tried hard not to cry. Nanny was very proud of me and told me so. She had just helped me to put on my Sunday dress and bonnet and I did not crease or make one mark on it.

Nanny had only intended to take me out for a little walk but, because I had been so brave, she decided to take me to visit her sister who lives in the sweetest little cottage with a thatched roof and tiny square windows. Nanny's sister always has a warm fire going in her cosy sitting-room. She calls it an Inglenook fireplace and the logs which burn on it smell so nice. Her husband is a woodman, he chops up logs from the trees and sells them in the village.

When we arrive Nanny's sister has toast ready for us which has been toasted on the open fire in the Inglenook. With the toast we have her home-made raspberry jam. I adore going to see her. Outside she keeps little rabbits in various pens. Her favourite rabbit, and my favourite too, is named Thumper because he thumps his paws against the wire netting when it is time for him to take his meals. He is fed with bran, and oats and milk. He is going to be a birthday present for a little boy in the village called Anthony.

Oh, I almost forgot to tell you, my name is Angela!

Francoise, Monique & Jacqueline

We three are always together. I don't really know why. Maybe because we all came from Paris. We love our friends in the attic, but they are so much bigger than we are. We are really tiny. Our names are Francoise, Monique and Jacqueline. Our dresses are pure silk trimmed with early Honiton lace. Jacqueline's dress and hat are really very fine and exquisite. The dress has a beautiful train at the back, which is also of Honiton lace, and there are tiny satin bows all over the skirt.

We simply adored living in Paris. We often talk about the olden days. On Sundays we would go to the Madeleine Church and watch the very smart ladies with great interest. After Church, we would buy flowers from a sweet old lady who sat on a chair at the top of the Church steps. She had little posies of violets and snowdrops or whatever was in season. We all loved this flower lady. She always had a smile for everyone. She had been there for years and she would always say "Good morning, what a lovely day", even if it was pouring with rain. We have often wondered what happened to her. We have been living in the attic for a very long time. We enjoy being here.

Monique says she liked Paris in the Spring when all the blossoms were out. She liked to walk along the Champs-Élysées and to see the beautiful shops along the Rue St-Honoré, the boats on the River Seine and the artists on the river bank.

Suzie & Janey

We thought we would like to do something quite different from our our friends, so my sister and I agreed to visit the Antique Market. We admired lots of pieces of furniture. Since our space in the attic is somewhat limited, we have chosen to show you our little wicker-backed chair. It also has a wicker-worked seat. It is exquisite and rather grand. Suzie says it is a William and Mary Chair. The dealer said it is late eighteenth century. Do you think a chair of that period would have cabriole legs? I don't really know. Nevertheless I know it is rather super in the attic. The antique dealer delivered it and put it in our part of the attic. He thought we lived in a magnificent house and we had to agree with him.

I do not know how many times I have had to remark to Suzie to fasten up her flannelette petticoat. It is always falling down. One day she will be completely embarrassed by it coming off altogether. All she has to do is tighten the tape around her waist. Oh dear, she is impossible. I expect I will have to do it for her – I thought so! "Janey, would you please tie up my petticoat?" she asks softly.

Sarah & Carole

Our names are Sarah and Carole. We have been friends for a long time. We have received an invitation to a Music Recital. It is going to be a very smart occasion. Rebecca has also received an invitation. We do hope she will be able to come along with us.

Our dresses have been made especially for tonight by Madame Saggers of Russell Square, London. She has been designing gowns since early in the 19th century. She is a perfect dressmaker. She also has a friend working with her who is a milliner – her hats are up to date in the latest styles.

We are longingly looking forward to the Recital. We hope the musicians will play "The Queen of Sheba" by Handel, "The Invitation to the Dance" by Strauss, and "The Sugar Plum Fairy" by Tchaikovsky – Carole is very fond of this piece. My favourite piece is "Bells Across the Meadow" by Albert Katellba. We both enjoy "Greensleeves" as arranged by Vaughan Williams.

At last we are about ready to go. My hair is very smart tonight. It is dark chestnut and so shiny. This style takes an age to arrange. It is very long – my hairdresser plaits it and piles it on top of my head in such an elegant manner, it remains like that for days.

Carole's hair is very blonde. White is not the colour for her to wear. I can wear any colour with my dark hair.

It is a long way to the Concert Hall. I must remember to tell our Coachman to collect Rebecca. She lives in the beautiful big old house called 'Bluebury Manor' in the next village.

Prunella

I designed my hat myself – that is why I insist you get a close look at it. It is my favourite hat. I am very fond of violets and daisies. There are lots of types of daisies in the garden where we live and, of course, the violets are found growing wild in the hedgerows. The flowers on my hat are artificial but a very good copy of the real ones.

My ear-rings are so special to me. They are antique. They were a present from Grandma. They actually belonged to her mother. I have pierced ears. Not many of my friends here have had their ears pierced.

Grandma also gave me the brooch I am wearing. It was a Christmas present. She always presents us all with jewellery on special occasions. Her favourite jewellery shop is in the High Street. It has a bow fronted window with tiny square glass panes. The owner, Mr Gold, is always cleaning the windows. He says the shop and windows get very dirty. It is because of all the horses and carriages going past at the great speed of 10 miles an hour. This, and the cobbled streets, creates dust.

Mr Gold is a very nice little man. He wears tiny glasses on the end of his nose. When he is talking to you he looks over his glasses, making him look so important. You would love his waistcoat. It is made of cream silk, delicately embroidered with tiny flowers of all colours. Sometimes he wears black velvet shoes with silver buckles on. The gold chain he wears on his waistcoat is fascinating. It is a very thick chain with a George III sovereign hanging from it in a little glass container.

Prunella has almost forgotten to pick up her purse. She usually only uses it when she goes to Church. It holds a small amount of money, and her tiny lorgnette. She doesn't really need these. She can see perfectly well without glasses – but at the moment they are the height of fashion.

Let's hope she remembers to take all the things she needs in the excitement of preparing for the Recital. It will be a great relief when we are all sitting down in the hall.

She enjoys lending her purse to her friends. They all admire it. Alexia, her cousin, often borrows it. Prunella knows Alexia will take great care of anything she borrows.

Oh no, Prunella! Have you forgotten your handkerchief as well as your purse.

I am so pleased you remembered where it was. It is such a pretty handkerchief. The lace is beautiful. Did you know it was made of Limerick lace and can also be worn as a cravat?

I know you don't need a cravat on your mauve dress. You could wear it with your lovely pink silk blouse and skirt. Do try it when we go out again.

Rebecca

Rebecca is so pretty. In fact, when Sarah, Carole and Rebecca are together, everyone looks and admires the three of them.

She is thinking perhaps the coachman will forget to call for her and go cantering by the house. That is why she has an anxious look in her eyes. She need not worry, her friends are so reliable, they have not forgotten.

Rebecca is wondering what music she enjoys most. I think she would like to hear the musicians play "The Song of the Two Cats" by Rossini. All one hears is "Meow, Meow" and so on. The music is very good.

Phoebe

Phoebe is staying at home this evening whilst Rebecca goes to the Recital. They are sisters and live together in a small portion of the attic.

Phoebe is embroidering a panel of tapestry and prefers to be alone. It is tedious work and requires a tremendous amount of concentration. The work is magnificent. It is of a peacock with his highly coloured tail displayed, standing by an old stone wall in the garden.

Phoebe intends to get the carpenter to make a pole so that she can hang it on the wall. It will certainly enhance the corner which they occupy.

Anorella

My friends went to the Recital last night. They are all discussing what went on. They certainly seemed to have had a wonderful time.

I cannot decide whether or not to go shopping with Virginia. My name is Anorella and we are sisters. I have decided I must go. I have to call on Madame Bourne to choose materials for my new dress. I think she is the best of dressmakers. Her patterns are superb, and her seamstress, who has worked for her for many years, produces perfect needlework.

This time I must instruct her to put the right amount of whale-bones in the bodice. The last dress she made for me had only one support in the back. It was very uncomfortable. I also like the look of the hooks and eyes – they look neat as fasteners.

Yes, I will go to town. I must remember to tell Annabel about the article I read in the magazine yesterday about 'Pears Soap'. Queen Charlotte used Pears soap for her complexion in the year AD 1788! This is perfectly true.

Virginia

Anorella is about to go shopping. She doesn't realise she has left her shopping list and bag on the kitchen table. I must look for her. She will be hopeless without her list.

Oh! There you are Anorella. I have thought of some more things you must buy. We need them for the kitchen and other places. Have you written down on your list Monkey Brand Soap for scrubbing the kitchen tables? Do not forget the Swan soap and the Sunlight soap for washing the clothes and linens. Also we need Ayers Sarsaparilla, Eno's Fruit Salts for headaches, and Dr. Ridges patent cook food for the infants – not forgetting the Allanbury Food for the bigger children.

I almost forgot, we also need some Clarkes Pyramid night lights.

"When Nights are dark,
Then think of Clarke,
Who's hit the mark
Precisely
For his Night Lights
Create Light Nights
In which you see
Quite nicely."

Pears Annual 1899.

Chapter
2

Away
We Go

Margarette & Maria

Margarette and Maria are going for a walk along the Glen. They collect and press wild flowers. Pressing flowers means putting them between the pages of old heavy books. When they are dry, they then put them into frames to make lovely pictures to hang on to the walls of the attic. They consider it to be an interesting hobby.

One of their favourites is the "Tufted Vetch", which is a pretty blue flower, it is actually a wild sweet pea. They are also fond of "The Bird's foot Trefoil", which is a glorious bright yellow. Then there is "Bind weed", which is a pretty white flower that dries very well. Also there are "Cowslips", "Celandine", "Crowfoot" (which is really a buttercup), "Violets" in pretty mauves, and "Red Poppies". These are the types of flowers they look for, along with numerous other varieties.

Margarette's dress is ivory silk taffeta with drapes of Chantilly lace, trimmed with caramel velvet. She is obviously going to change into her walking dress.

Maria's dress is delicate fine cotton with small pin tucks around the hem, and a petticoat trimmed with broderie Anglaise lace. Maria is wearing her sweet little black suede boots – they are strong and ideal for walking.

Pavla & Charlotte

Whilst other people are collecting wild flowers or going to parties and concerts, I am going to school. Mummie is taking me to Miss Wild who teaches small children. It isn't really a school day today – at least no lessons.

We are having our prize day. I am in the infants class. We play with a bat and ball. Older children play with a hoop and stick. I cannot do this because I can't run very fast and I do not wish to get my new boots dirty.

I do not really know if I am about to receive a prize. If I do, I would like it to be the book called "Merry Playmates". It is one of "The Little Folks Picture Books". It costs a lot of money – one shilling and sixpence.

Mummie says if I do not receive a prize, she will reward me with one. She say she is very pleased with my work. She thinks I have worked very hard with my lessons. She prefers the book called "Birdies Message".

Mummie recites this little poem to me:

Birdie and the Cherries
Pretty Birdie and the Little Bell,
Cherries Ripe you love so well,
Cherries rosy round and sweet
June has brought you both a treat.

Mummie's name is Pavla. My name is Charlotte.

Toby

I wish I could go to school with Charlotte. It is a long way to walk. Very soon I will be able to walk. My Victorian walker is a tremendous help, it is on china castors. I enjoy it. I can go very fast, especially when I push myself around. At the moment it is rather difficult and hard work on the carpet. I am normally in the nursery. We do not have a carpet there.

Today we are having guests, that is why I have this clean white dress on. My name is Toby. Little boys wear this type of clothing until they are twelve months old.

My gollywog is very independent. He is much older than I am. Some years ago he belonged to another little boy, who grew up and was too old to own Golly. Now he is mine and I adore him. He is my greatest comfort, especially when we are alone. I tell him all my secrets.

My secret today is that I want to hurry up and grow to be a big boy, then I can go to school with my sister Charlotte.

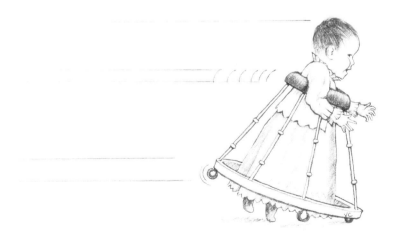

Annette

I think the old saying "A woman's work is never done", is perfectly true. Fridays come and go so quickly, this is the day I polish my furniture. My name is Annette.

The chest of drawers which you can see is now beautifully polished, is in fact much older than myself. It was here in 1880. It belonged to an old Aunt, who took tremendous care of all the family possessions. The dinner service also belonged to her, it consists of 120 pieces.

She actually made and mixed her very own furniture polish. She made it with Beeswax turpentine to which sometimes she would add a little of oil of lavender. It was a refreshing perfume that penetrated around the house.

Prudence & Mabel

Prudence is a very vain person, even to walk along the country lane she must wear her Sunday best dress.

She is showing off. Who does she think she is? We are the best of friends, but at times her behaviour and actions can be extremely exasperating.

She walks elegantly along, insisting that I open the gate. In the most nonchalant way she says "Mabel, open the gate, I cannot or I will soil my dress". Notice, she always forgets to say please. Tomorrow I will wear my best dress, it will then be her turn to open the gate.

It is necessary to open and close the gate each time we leave the drive. Mr Humber, the farmer who lives down the lane, has two working horses. If they get the chance, they come into the garden, especially the kitchen garden, and eat the vegetables: Brussels sprouts, beans, peas, cabbages; all these and any other things they can find. They create a lot of damage in a very short time.

The gate is very heavy and difficult to open. The gardener periodically puts oil on to the hinges which makes it easier, but rather messy.

Hetty

I am Hetty the head cook. I work for Miss Prudence and Miss Mabel. They are very good and kind, although I prefer Miss Mabel – she is the more understanding of the two.

I have tidied and swept up the kitchen. Soon Miss Prudence will be back from her walk, then she will give me her orders for cooking the dinner tonight. I believe we are expecting guests. I have a kitchen maid to help me. At the moment she is in the Dairy churning the cream to make butter for the week. We make our own cheese.

Of course, we also have the task of making the bread, scones, teacakes and even oatcakes in the winter.

As I thought; the orders for dinner tonight are as follows – 12 people at the table, that is including Miss Prudence and Miss Mabel.

The Menu is:-

Mock Turtle Soup
Codfish Oyster Sauce, with stewed Eels
Haunch of Venison, or Saddle of Mutton
Widgeon or Pheasant
Cabinet Pudding
Apricot Tartlets

Wines:
Hock and Champagne

Before dinner, tea is served in the Drawing Room at 4 o'clock precisely. It will just be cinnamon toast and China tea with sliced lemon today.

Betty

The church bells are ringing. It is Sunday once again. All the village people go to church. It is a lovely old church with stained glass windows which the sun shines through. At the end of the church is a font where the little babies are baptised.

The seats and pews are magnificently carved. The ladies in the village take turns to polish them. The scent from the polish travels throughout the church. It is very pleasant when entering. It reminds me of a Convent I once knew, where the Nuns spent their time polishing and cleaning.

I am a dressmaker and I come from Wales. All my sewing materials are put away on a Sunday. My faithful sewing machine needs a rest just like me.

My sewing is mainly done for the lady who lives in the big hall in the village. She is so generous. She gave me the material to make the woollen dress I am now wearing. The shawl is handwoven. The whole outfit is very warm to wear. I have a money bag, which I keep under my black apron. It is sewn on to a cotton belt. It will hold three gold sovereigns or six half sovereigns.

I have my name on a tape fastened to the belt, "Betty", just in case it gets lost. Everyone in the village knows 'Betty the Dressmaker'.

Harriet & Hannah

Harriet and Hannah are in deep conversation. They are undecided whether they should go to the races or be content with a walk in the park. A walk in the park is the final decision. Harriet likes to watch the horse-riders cantering and galloping along the paths. The ladies ride side-saddle, wearing superb immaculate tunics, in either dark green, black, brown or maroon, and top hats with chiffon bands around, flying as they go by.

It is a glorious day, the birds are singing. The chaffinches, the little robins and the house martins are all busy building their nests. There is a tiny yellow hammer with his fine yellow feathers, he sings so sweetly. Also we see a wagtail who is kept so busy wagging his tail, Hannah wonders why he never tires.

Nurses and Nannies in their smart uniforms are taking the children for their daily walk. Their prams are beautiful. We have several lovely prams here in the attic, exactly the same type and style as those we see in the park.

Wendy

Wendy had been asked by Harriet and Hannah to join them on their walk. She did want to join them, in fact she went part of the way, but then she automatically turned off down a little street where she knows of a shop that sells antique china. She collects Willow Pattern plates. She knows a great deal about the design and the stories attached to the history of the illustrations. The plates have willow trees hanging near a bridge. On the bridge there are little people walking over, and birds flying above them.

Wendy's favourite colour is blue. She calls it Royal Blue, just like the colour on the plates. That is the reason she is wearing blue straps on her shoes, a blue bow on her dress and a very smart blue hat. She has very fascinating blue eyes.

Aunt Sophia

Aunt Sophia has prepared tea. She is awaiting her two nieces. They should be arriving very soon. They are Martha and Matilda.

The morning has been so hectic for Aunt Sophia. The teas she serves are something special, hot muffins with butter and cream, seed cake and Madeira cake with home-made apricot jam, or preserve as she describes it. She really enjoys friends and relations calling on her.

Aunt Sophia was born in Germany. From there she was transported to the World's Exhibition in Chicago, America. There she was put on to a doll stand. A lady bought her as a present for her little daughter. She remained in America for many years.

She travelled around America, going to Florida. She stayed in Baltimore. At one time she lived in a log cabin by the lakes. She finally settled down in Massachusetts in a little town called 'Strawberry Banke', Portsmouth, New Hampshire. This is the town where settlers arrived in the year 1630. They had not had fresh food for many weeks. Here they found the place covered with wild strawberries growing beside the banks of the river. Hence the name 'Strawberry Banke', but in the year of 1653 it was renamed Portsmouth. Aunt Sophia adores telling us this story, which is really true.

Some years later she was brought to England by an English lady. She then came to live in the attic. She says it is her favourite home. She finds it very peaceful and has so many kind friends who appreciate and are thrilled by her stories and unusual adventures.

Anita

This horse belongs to a friend of mine who is a farmer. He lives down the lane and delivers milk twice a day to the big house.

We usually feed the horse with oats, but today he is content with some fresh grass that I have found for him. He is very lovely but so mischievous. His name is Mercury. He has that name because he will canter and run and jump around his paddock. He is so fast, he is almost impossible to catch. He hates standing still, consequently it is necessary to hold him tight by his reins, otherwise he would run away.

I am not properly dressed to be holding Mercury, but I was on my way to visit Aunt Sophia. She is having one of her outstanding afternoon tea parties. She hasn't really invited me but she is always delighted to see me. My name is Anita. I am a friend of Aunt Sophia's nieces Martha and Mildred.

Cecilia

There is a tremendous amount of activity going on around me. Mummies are dressing their children and everyone is having an amusing time. They are all smartening themselves up to go to tea-parties, picnics, etc. I sincerely hope they all have a wonderful day. My bed is conveniently placed at an angle in the corner, so I am able to observe all the action.

My name is Cecilia. I was found on a stall in Portobello Road in London in 1950. I came from Germany in 1895. I belonged to a family where there were four little girls. They were very kind to me and, as you may observe, I am still in perfect condition. We travelled a great deal. In fact, when I belonged to the youngest little girl, she went to Switzerland and insisted on taking me with her. We lived there for several years. It is a really beautiful country. I adored the mountains in the spring, and seeing the wild flowers, the edelweiss and the bright red and yellow poppies, blowing in the breeze. The winters, though, were very hard and cold. There were deep falls of snow and ice on the windows.

Urita

Urita is the little coloured doll in the centre. She is telling us all a story. She is so fascinating. It is exciting when we are alone, we tell each other about our lives before we came to live in the attic.

Urita's grandfather worked on a sugar plantation in the Caribbean Islands. The men and women had to work extremely hard in the hot climate, earning very little money. They cut the sugar canes down and loaded them on to trucks to go to the sugar factories where they were processed before being sold in England and other countries. The sugar is a delicious dark brown. Most white people do not realise how hard and dirty the work is. The plantation workers are in the sugar fields for many hours each day. They are very happy people. They sing all day long.

On another island called Tobago, lived an Uncle. He earned his living by growing bananas and coconuts. Each Friday they would carry the bananas on their heads down to the wharf. Here they were put on to the boats, these also came to England.

As they loaded the bananas and coconuts in to the boats, the natives would sing their favourite boat songs. It was difficult to understand the words of the song, because when they were together they spoke in what we call Pidgin English.

Tessa & Tiny

These two are what we call the Whimsical Twins. We actually call them Tweedle-dee and Tweedledum. Their real names are Tessa and Tiny. Every morning they sit as sedately as possible and have their morning cup of coffee together.

Tweedledee is frightfully absent minded, she forgets just everything. She gets so thoroughly mixed up. Look, she has put the tea-pot on the table instead of the coffee pot. "Thank goodness! We haven't any guests for coffee this morning", says Tweedledum. "Tweedledee, you are completely and absolutely impossible. All you can do is smile. I suppose I will have to accept you as you really are."

Velocipede Horse

I was made in the year 1870. For years I lived in an old shed in a farmyard. I was then in a very dilapidated condition, having played with so many little children. I was broken and had no wheels. I thought my owner was about to throw me on to a rubbish heap, when someone suggested I should be put in one of the London Sale Rooms, as I was so old and was regarded as a collector's piece. I was really unbelievably unhappy. I only had one wheel, no saddle and my paintwork was unrecognisable.

So, I was sent to London. Here my luck changed, when a very kind young gentleman called Mark bought me. I know I cost a large sum of money, in spite of my faults.

When I got back to Mark's home, he put me in a little house for a long time. I thought, oh dear, I have been forgotten again. Then suddenly, I heard Mark discussing with David, a carpenter, how I could be restored and repainted. He found two wheels from Wendy's antique shop for my back legs, then Mark made the lovely leather saddle. The one thing they couldn't find was a chain that could stretch from the handles on my head, through my body to the back wheels. It is possible for me to be pushed around without the chain, although I am no longer a toy.

Now I live in the attic. Mark says I will live for another hundred years. Today my friends the otter and squirrel have accompanied me out into the garden.

Teddy & Pinky Kendell

Teddy and Pinky have lived in the attic for a few years. Previous to this they belonged to a little girl named Mary. She is now grown-up and was delighted to find friends for them in the attic. They do not forget Mary. They write to her sometimes. They miss her and her sweet little cottage where she lives, somewhere near Stratford-on-Avon, the place where Shakespeare was born.

This is the last letter they wrote and Mr Gollywog posted it:

The Attic,
The Big Old House

Dear Mary,

Pinky and I are sending you a photograph, with all our devotion, to let you see how we love our new home. We have made many friends. In fact, Pinky has found a lovely little girl friend. It is really a great secret but we can tell you, she is a charming small white lamb. She is called Pretty Sue because Pinky thinks she is pretty. She has a beautiful delicate white coat (at the moment it is looking a little grubby).

We are going for a ride in the garden on Mr Bendit's cart. The horse's name is Dobbin. He is a chestnut colour. On the front of the cart are painted these words. U. BENDIT and on the back is W. E. MENDIT. Isn't that funny? We think so.

Mr Bendit said: "Teddy Kendell you may borrow my cart to take your friends for a ride, but you must be back by sundown." I did not know anything about sundown but March Hare did, he said "It means we must be home before dark". Anyway Dobbin the old horse said he must be back very soon to have his meal of oats and bran. He is always hungry.

In the picnic basket we have carrots for March Hare, fresh grass and lettuce for Pretty Sue, and what do you think for Pinky and I? – Honey and Ovaltine to drink.

Pretty Sue belonged to a little girl name Emmie.

With all our love,
Teddy and Pinky Kendell.

Constance

I have a new bicycle so today I have decided to take my baby doll for a ride. The basket is for shopping, but it can be used for very small dolls.

I am riding into the village to collect the daily papers as well as my very own paper called "The Childrens Newspaper". I collect it each week. It has very exciting stories on travel, puzzles and lots of school news. It helps me with my school lessons such as history and geography. Miss Hubbard, the owner of the shop, always writes my name on the paper – "Miss Constance".

I also buy sweets and biscuits for my friends. Miss Hubbard is a dear old lady. She has had the shop for many years. She lives alone, apart from her pets. Her dog is called Spot. He is black with a huge white spot on the middle of his head. She also has a cat called Ginger. She says he is a tremendous help to her. He is very good and chases the mice away from the sugar and flour bags.

In the village there are two little dogs who are great friends of Spot. They all go to see Mr Lamb, the village butcher. Spot's friends are called Fleet and Sultan. Sometimes they meet another friend called Bumbles, and they all go together. Mr Lamb gives them each a lovely big bone.

Pamela, Linda, Caron & Rebecca

Linda, Caron and Rebecca are supposed to be reading their story books. In fact, they are deep in discussion as to who is the next to have a ride on Topper.

Pamela's riding time is now over. It is Linda's turn next. Every afternoon we have our playtime, if we have been good during the morning. We pretend we are going to London to see the King and Queen. It is great fun because we make Topper gallup very fast, but he never gets to London – Rocking Horses never do, but it is great fun to imagine we are in London.

Bridget & Belinda

Bridget joins the children from the attic, to go to Miss Wilds' School. She is in the big girls classroom. Some smaller dolls from the attic are in the Nursery classroom. Bridget is very kind, her greatest kindness is towards her baby sister, Belinda.

Mummie is making a cake for their tea. They are waiting to see it come out of the oven. Bridget adores the delicious smell of the baking of cakes and bread.

After tea and before their bedtime, Bridget will tell Belinda a nursery story and about the lessons she has to do at school.

Fennella & Francesca

These two ladies are classed as 'Boudoir Dolls'. They were made to adorn a ladies bedroom, or the boudoir, which may be the drawing room.

Fennella and Francesca are great friends and have been for years. They lived with a lady in France. During the 1914 war, when people were evacuated from France, some came to England. Fennella and Francesca were packed in a trunk by their owner and she brought them to England with her. They have remained here ever since.

As you can imagine, their wardrobes contain magnificent dresses, hats and shoes all designed and made by Mme Emmeline Raymonde. Their clothes have been treated with tremendous care and today they look so smart. They are so precise in every arrangement they make and always wear beautiful hats with each outfit.

Today they intend to go to their favourite little cafe to meet their very dear friend Chloe and to enjoy coffee and patisseries together. The birds in the cage have been with them for a long time. Often Francesca lets them fly around, they are very tame and know when to return to their cage. The cage is made of brass and requires patience to clean and polish. It was found on an antique stall in the flea market in Paris.

Chapter
3

Little
People's
Houses

Victorian Houses

This is an early Victorian House, in magnificent condition. It is large and spacious. There are five big rooms: a lovely drawing room, two bedrooms, dining room, and kitchen. One bedroom is made into a nursery. At the top of the house is the attic – this has been made into two bedrooms.

There is quite a large family living here, so all the available space is required. Actually, the attic bedrooms are very comfortable. The floors are covered with thick carpet and each room has a four-poster bed inside.

From the hall a door takes you into the conservatory, which is full of flowers and tropical plants. It is so restful in there and, of course, it faces South.

St. Pauls Villa

Years ago this dolls house belonged to a little girl named Lydia. Her father was a Vicar and lived at St. Pauls Villa, situated in the village near his church.

St. Pauls Villa is an exact copy of the family house and this is where Lydia was born.

One day she discovered the house in the attic. It had been there for a long time and completely forgotten.

After this her little friends played with it, and naturally over the years it sadly became damaged. It is now perfect. A very clever carpenter and builder repaired it, altered the rooms slightly and re-decorated the exterior.

Lydia wanted the house to be where little children would see it and appreciate it. Grandma says it will remain here for ever and we must always thank Miss Lydia for presenting her dolls house to us.

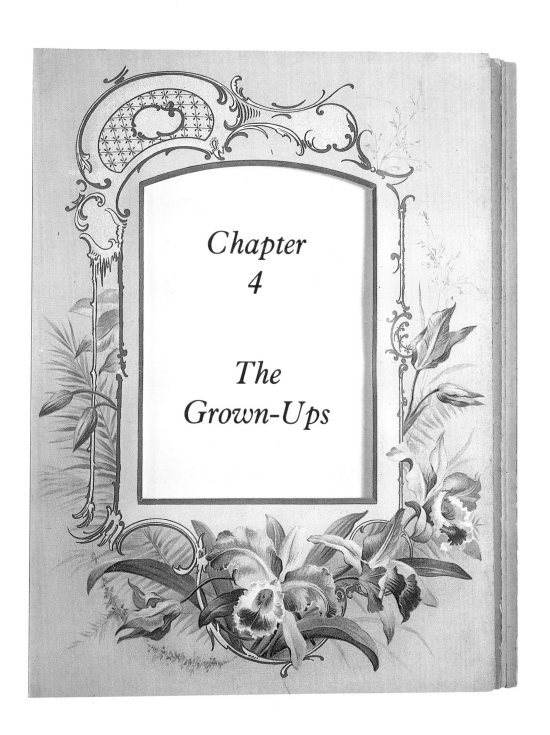

Chapter
4

The
Grown-Ups

Petula

Petula is modelling this wonderful little dress. It is white lawn with insertions of lace edged with embroidery in tiny white flowers. It also has small pin-tucking around the skirt, sleeves and bodice, and pink ribbons threaded through the waist. The petticoats underneath match up with the same design.

The dressing table is 18th Century, the chair also the same period, it has a beautiful original tapestry seat, but as Cecilia is occupying it you cannot see the cover.

The little silver dressing table set and the small picture frames are Georgian.

Camille & Joseph

My brother and I are going to see elephants, donkeys and many other animals of all kinds at the circus on the Village Green. We have been once before on my brother's birthday. We saw a funny little clown who jumped around and squirted water at us from a huge water pistol almost as big as himself. I do hope we see him again today, his name is Norman. My name is Camille and my brother's name is Joseph.

The dress I am wearing today is Victorian. I adore the cape, it ties around the neck with pink ribbons that form a sweet little bow at the front. My brother's suit is a sailor's outfit. It has a label in it 'Made by Brights, Bournemouth' "Sailors Rowe" year 1920.

Anthony

Anthony has lost his white stockings. His mother tells him to look in the clothes trunk – he is sure to find them there.

The suit he is wearing is for parties only. He has a blue velvet jacket with tiny pewter buttons down each side. His trousers are ivory satin and around his waist he wears a wide silk cummerbund fastened with minute pearl buttons at the back. Around his neck he has a lace jabot, fastened with a diamond brooch that once belonged to Grandma.

Anthony adores his cat whose name is Tinkle. He loves to go for a walk in the fields. Tinkle is quite old. He has the most beautiful eyes. In fact, Anthony thinks Louis Wain, who draws both funny and vivid impressions of cats, should use Tinkle as his model. Louis Wain likes to teach children to do his drawings.

Jeremy & Wilhelmina

Jeremy and Wilhelmina are going to a ball. It is to be held in aid of a children's charity fund. It is going to be very exciting because the King and Queen will be there to open it.

The Prince and Princess will start the dancing. Wilhelmina has a dance card and her partners must book a dance with her. Each writes his name down on her card with her gold pencil which has a diamond on. She then knows who she will be dancing with during the evening. She looks so beautiful, Jeremy thinks the handsome Prince will ask her to dance.

Her dress is white gauze with embroidery all over the skirt and bodice, trimmed with Valenciennes lace. The cape is Edwardian ivory cashmere wool having a shorter cape attached, with panels of embroidery trimmed with Brussels lace. Jeremy's cream, satin suit is of the same period. These two outfits have always been very carefully kept together over the years.

Anthony is going to the party with them. If he can find his white stockings!

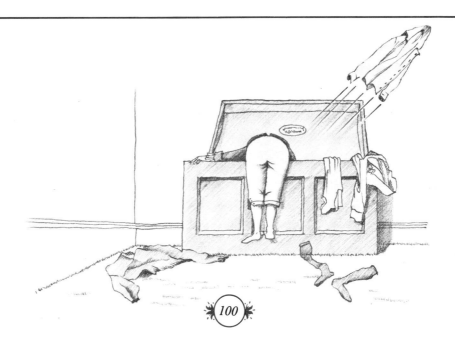

Aunt Letitia

Aunt Letitia is very elegant. Her dress is the most desirable one in the attic.

It is mauve moire silk with yards and yards of material in the skirt. Her waist measures sixteen inches.

I cannot say much more, except I must remark on her shoes. They are so small, made of heavy satin, decorated with diamonds, pearls and rubies.

You will see more of her as you read on.

Rose

The ladies of the attic are so breathtaking. We just stop and look at them, I have the feeling they know of their beauty. We do not ask them where they are going to, or what they are going to do, they seem to be really grown-up.

This is Rose, she and Letitia always arrange their outings togcthcr. Their dresses are immaculate and so superb.

They must be going to a party. They have special hair-styles that indicate something exciting ahead. Very outstanding, wouldn't you think?

Letitia is discussing the day's outing with Rose. There is an excellent exhibition at the National Art Gallery. They are both very interested in oil paintings and have a tremendous appreciation of English art.

They have decided to go to the Vernon Gallery. On entering, they are confronted by superb marble statues and ornaments of great interest and education.

Most of the paintings in the Vernon Gallery were painted before the reign of Henry VIII.

Letitia enjoyed the paintings at the gallery. Her great interest was seeing the portraits of influential people by Sir Joshua Reynolds, Gainsborough and Rubens. Rose's opinions differ on various paintings. She finds landscapes far more appealing than portraits.

"The Village Festival" by Wilkie is without doubt her favourite. She likes the sunshine, the ladies in their bright dresses and the lovely old rustic inn with the innocent children playing around in the yard.

Another of her favourite paintings is Constable's "Cornfield" with the laden cart and the old horse going down the lane, the autumn tinted trees, and the faithful dog. There is a boy gathering boughs from the trees at the edge of the wood. Rose thinks it all looks so real.

Emmeline

The Regimental Ball is to be held in the Assembly Rooms at the Headquarters. Lady Emmeline has a written invitation on a pink and gold card.

She is very excited and longing to attend. As you see she is looking full of confidence and supreme. Actually, she is shaking like a leaf and feeling very unsure of herself.

Lady Emmeline has met her escort only once before. He is so charming and she secretly adores him, which accounts for her nervousness. The young officer is dressed in a red uniform jacket, fastened with brightly polished regimental buttons and his black trousers have braid down each side of the legs. He has a cloak hanging from one shoulder and a sword hanging from his belt – he looks so handsome in his immaculate uniform.

He is waiting at the main entrance door for Lady Emmeline to appear. The coachman has the door of the barouche open, ready for them to enter.

The evening is going to be wonderful. They will dance the Quadrille and other dances, and have a romantic dinner. The hall will be decorated with the regimental colours. There will be pictures of the King and Queen and around the room will be military trophies, with the French and English flags draped on the walls.

Catalina

Catalina and Victoria were going to the Opera at the Haymarket, but decided against that since they have heard there is to be a grand piano recital at the Adelphia Hall.

There is to be a special pianist. He is well known. This is his first visit to the Adelphia. His name is Johna Kinkel.

The music he will be playing is by Beethoven, Bach, Chopin and Mendlessohn, whose latest piece is "The Venetian Gondola Song".

Music has become fashionable in Society. Today each drawing room has a piano for recital parties after dinner.

Catalina owns a piano, but it is Victoria who is the pianist.

Aunt Victoria's Dress

What has happened to Aunt Victoria's head? We cannot believe it, Aunt Victoria without her head!

It was often said, and we always laughed, whenever we overheard Catalina remark, "Victoria, one day you will lose your head!"

"Don't be stupid Eliza, that is the model Aunt Victoria uses to put her precious dresses on. They are so valuable, she cannot hang them in her wardrobe. The model is to keep them in shape. Normally she has a cover over the dress – that is why they go unnoticed. She is wearing her black dress tonight, that is why it stands uncovered. She is going to the piano recital."

"But you must admit it does look amusing. One would think her head had actually come off and disappeared, the model looks so real", replied Eliza.

Chapter
5

In the
Garden

Alexia

My cousin Prunella suggested that I borrow her little purse to match my dress. It is made of the tiniest little beads one could possibly find. It has a small chain of real silver for the handle.

Prunella also owns another purse. At the moment she cannot find it, I think it is possibly in the old chest along with a host of other small antique objects. When she can find it, she says I may keep this one.

It is so refreshing to have the time to spend an afternoon in the garden. This afternoon I heard the Cuckoo. He sings a little song that goes something like this, 'In July away I fly. In August away I must Cuckoo, Cuckoo.'' It is the sign of the beginning of summer when he is around, and a lovely time of the year.

My dress is made of white organza, with dots of black velvet worked on to the material, trimmed with pink velvet ribbons and edged with exquisite black Chantilly lace.

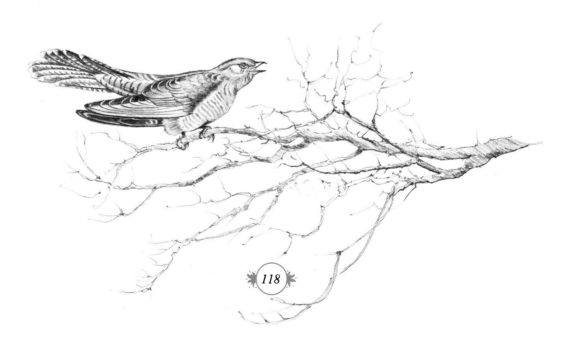

Alicia & Her Mummie

Alicia and her Mummie are going to walk through the park. At the moment they are by the old oak door at the side of our big house. They have just arrived from the attic.

Only in Alice's dream could the pram be carried down from the attic, because, like the other prams you will see, they are all so big and very heavy.

The old door opens onto a magnificent garden. There are lovely roses, beautiful flowers of every type, also an interesting herb garden.

You will see a number of our friends from the attic walking around the terraces and paths of the garden. You will no doubt enjoy looking at them and all their magnificent dresses. Mummie's dress is for the afternoons. It is made of pure silk material. It is lovely, with flowers hand-painted all over. There is a long train at the back that drags along the ground. It is pale pink silk. There are layers and layers of petticoats. This enables the dress to hang so perfectly.

There is also a handbag on the side of the pram which is embroidered to match the dress.

Petra, Patricia & Pauline

It is really a wonderful, wonderful day. We are so happy to be in the position to have an afternoon out of doors. The birds are singing. We have seen a little squirrel – he had a small apple in his hands. He was sitting under the tree, nibbling away at his apple. He saw us watching him. He obviously didn't appreciate this, so he just scampered away down the drive. He and his friends trespass in the orchard. The gardener, Thomas, gets very annoyed. He says Cook will not get any apples this year.

We know it is very warm. We do not need our cloaks or hats on, but we insisted on wearing them to enable you all to see how beautiful they really are.

Our names are Petra, Patricia and Pauline. We are three sisters.

Patricia and Pauline are looking for the deer. There are a great number in the park. There are two kinds, the fallow deer which are white with light brown spots on. Then we have the red deer. They are huge and coloured brown. Very often they will wander almost to the wall, but unfortunately, not today.

Dorothy & Doreen

Dorothy and Doreen are admiring the lilies. They have a heavenly scent, especially in the evenings. Dorothy says she would love to take some back to the attic. This is impossible because when Alice's dream is over, we are all dolls again and, therefore, there isn't anyone in the attic to look after the flowers.

Annabel

I am Annabel. I have lost my friends Dorothy and Doreen. It is really my fault. I walk so slowly and keep stopping to admire everything around me, I even find the lawns fascinating. It is exactly like walking on a green carpet. Do you know they actually call me 'Slow Coach'. My friends do not realise I will have lots more to talk about when we all return to the attic.

They are obviously looking for me in another part of the garden. The parks and grounds are so huge, it is almost impossible to find each other.

As you might gather Dorothy's dress is made of the same material as mine, heavy silk satin with small white beads sewn on to represent flowers. The sleeves, bodice and skirt are trimmed with very delicate lace.

I am wearing the smartest little Victorian bonnet, tied and decorated with pink baby ribbons.

Valerie

This is Valerie. She has a wonderful complexion. Her face is made of fine porcelain. She also has immaculate features. Her smartness is extreme and she wears her clothes very well, taking great care to have the right accessories.

The dress she is wearing today is exquisite, made of pure silk with a huge collar hanging over her shoulders. It is trimmed with fine Honiton lace.

Over her dress she is wearing an ivory coloured cloak. Down the back is a panel of embroidered little squares with small flowers in the centre. The cloak is lined with silk identical to that of the dress. Her hat is cream felt, with a huge cabbage rose on the front.

Valerie refuses to turn around, so I am sorry you cannot see the back of the outfit. I must add, all her clothes are a family heirloom, they have been worn by little girls some years ago. Valerie is so proud of the opportunity to wear them. She would like you to know that her boots are made of white kid leather, with tiny buckles on the front.

Olivia

Olivia has been watching the butterflies flying high and low on the herbaceous borders. She saw a beautiful Red Admiral, it looked so regal with the sun shining on its wings, showing up the transparent colour of red.

Coming over from the kitchen garden was another type of butterfly, with wings of white and a slight tinge of yellow. This is called a Cabbage White Butterfly.

Olivia's hand and face are made of wax. It is not advisable for her to stay in the sun a moment too long, it would be tragic if the sun melted her face.

On the way back to the attic, she will walk through the rose garden. These are her favourite flowers, in particular she likes the old tree of moss roses that grows in the corner right underneath the attic window.

Carmen & Katie

This is our second set of twins. The first two are Tweedledee and Tweedledum. Now we have Carmen and Katie. They were actually made in Egypt, but after living in the attic for many years they now wear English dresses.

They have dressed themselves up today in some lovely clothes they have found in the old travelling trunk in the corner of the attic.

Carmen's dress is made of pink flannelette, with layers of broad Irish lace around the hem, whilst Katie's dress is made of lawn and broderie Anglaise lace, hand-stitched and embroidered.

They are returning from the herb garden. You will always find a herb garden in old English homes, outside of course! There is a terrific fragrant scent in this particular garden and so many species for the kitchen. We have parsley, sage, thyme, sorrel and angelica. For making medicines there is sarsaparilla, red clover, burdock and, lastly, which we all love for making pot-pourri, is sweet woodruff, sweet marjoram, lavender, lemon mint and so many, many more.

Loretta & Lorna

Loretta and Lorna have walked a long way from the gardens. They find themselves in a field quite a distance away.

They are so thrilled, they have found a real Romany Gypsy with his caravan. He has allowed them to peep inside. They were amazed to see two bunk beds, a table with seats at the side, a lovely old brass kettle shining in the sun, and so many attractive pieces of china – Crown Derby plates, Staffordshire figures, Royal Doulton cups and saucers, and old Jasper Wedgwood bowls and dishes.

The Gypsy man is doing the cooking, whilst his wife and two children are going around the cottages in the village selling clothes pegs, which are used to hang washing out to dry on the clothes line on wash days. These pegs are made by the Gypsies themselves from the branches of the willow trees.

Another way the Gypsies make their money is to tell fortunes. The lady Gypsy knocks on your door, when you open it to her she will say, "Cross my palm with silver and I will tell you your fortune." You then give her a sixpenny or threepenny silver piece.

Magdeline

My name is Magdeline. I am the nursemaid for Matti. She is very easy to care for. I find her very well behaved and also great company. When I take her out of her pram, she enjoys trying to pull up the grass.

I lived in Ireland for twenty-five years. My home was in Killarney. When my owner moved to another country, most of her belongings were put into an Auction Sale, including me, and a gentleman bought me. The next day I was in his shop window with a price ticket pinned on to my dress. I hated that and felt so unhappy. I was in that window for three weeks. It seemed a terribly long time, and how I loathed all the people who stared at me from the pavement.

One day a very pleasant young man came into the shop. He had a lovely smile. I liked him immediately. He said he wanted to include me in a collection. He brought me back to England. We travelled on a big boat which rocked around in the sea.

I was finally put into the attic with the collection. I didn't know what 'collection' meant. Now I do know, I am with all these wonderful friends and exciting toys. I adore being here and I am so thankful the kind young gentleman rescued me from that antique shop.

Matti

Magdeline knows I like this particular part of the garden – the heather is a beautiful mauve colour and grows very high. There are various types of heather in the rock gardens, some pale lavender and some very dark. My favourite is the pretty pink.

Often on our walks we pick blackberries for Cook. She makes delicious jams, blackberry and apple, and also blackberry jelly. These two are so popular, they taste really nice. Cook also makes tarts and puts the jam in to them. We all enjoy these. We have to walk to the wood to collect the berries.

Magdeline says it is too far to go to the woods today, so we will be more than content to stay in the gardens. She says we can gather blackberries in Alice's next dream.

Alethea

I was discovered in a sale room in London. My owner says I was not expensive because at that time it was not in vogue to collect toys and dolls.

Anyhow, my name is Alethea. I looked like a real little ragamuffin at one time, but when my hair was cleaned and my arms and legs were restored, I looked just as you see me now. This garden is literally full of prams and baby dolls.

We do not interfere with each other's afternoon happiness. We are each finding different things to do.

My Nanny and I are going to gather flowers.

See, Nanny has given me some orange blossom which she found on the tree which was too high for me to reach. Orange Blossom is so pretty and has a glorious perfume.

We have a long afternoon and I am allowed to be out of my pram which I enjoy.

Nanny says we will have time to go for a walk along the country lane. The flowers here in the garden are beautiful, but secretly I prefer the wild flowers, especially the wild violets. I also like primroses and forget-me-knots.

We will go through the woods that lead on to the lane, and at this time of the year we will see the bluebells scattered around.

Mandy

There is a village fair today. Several of us will be going. It is always great fun. All the village people arrive with their children.

The little girls always look so sweet. They wear clean white dresses and very pretty straw hats, with little coloured flowers around them, tied on with pink, blue or even red ribbons.

There will be the man with the barrel organ. He dresses up like an Italian Gypsy wearing ear-rings and a red scarf with white spots on. He has the sweetest little monkey who dances on the top of the organ. He is dressed in red. His name is "Kiki". I know, because he has his name written on his hat. After each piece of music the organ grinder has played, Kiki comes around the audience with a little red bag to collect money.

There is also a baby show. Nanny says she will put me in to it. I hope she doesn't really mean what she says, I know I will cry if she does.

My name is Mandy.

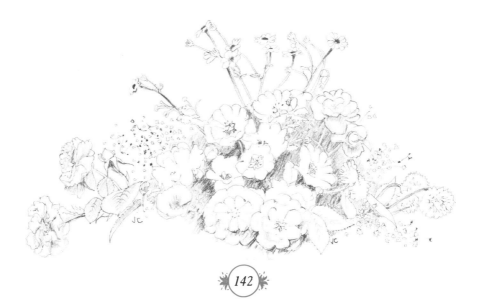

Mary

Although I was made in Japan, would it surprise you to know I was found in Baltimore in America?

I just do not know how I arrived in America. I wasn't at all happy although America is a beautiful place to live, and the people are very kind, but my life there was so dull. I was in an old Junk Shop, situated on a very lonely road away from everyone. I was pushed in a corner getting dustier and dirtier every week. I felt so untidy and forlorn.

One day a car stopped outside. This was unusual. The lady came inside and bought me. I think she must have felt very sorry for me, because I heard her say to the man in the shop that he was asking too much money for me. I was so happy when she finally said she would buy me.

She brought me back to England with her. It was a very long journey. After a few weeks she made my very smart dress and put me in this extremely elegant pram. I could not believe what was happening. My home is now in the attic, and I have so many friends – it is all so romantic, after years of unhappiness and loneliness.

My name is Mary because I was found in Maryland.

This is me again, Mary. It is wonderful to be sitting in the grass, although I am very proud to be in my pram.

I am waiting for Alethea. She is with her Nanny gathering wild flowers. She will be coming this way. We are going to make daisy chains. I have taken my bonnet off, so I can put a daisy chain around my head. It will take twenty daisies fastened together to go round. I know, because Alethea and I have made daisy chains before.

I did not see any daisies growing when I lived in Baltimore, but then I wasn't ever taken for a walk in the country.

My dress is really a nightdress. It is very pretty. It has been altered to make a day dress. It is made of fine linen and is so white it almost shines in the sun. It has yards and yards of broderie Anglaise lace around the bottom. The same is continued on the two petticoats I am wearing underneath.

I have a flannelette robe to match my bonnet, it is magnificently embroidered.

George

I am what one calls a character doll. My name is George. My face is is modelled to represent a real baby. They say I am an excellent copy, but I will be so pleased when my hair grows. The sun is so very hot. I wish Nanny would put on my bonnet! I know she is going to take me out of my pram to have my photograph taken lying down, so you can see my lovely dress. It will not take long, then I may have my bonnet on and be out of the sun.

Chin Chini

Alice says I am the star of the attic. This makes me feel very happy. I am sure the reason is that I have not got an English face. My features are Chinese, and I know all little English girls have a lovely fascination for dolls like me, because of our colour, small eyes and tiny flat noses.

But really, in spite of all this, I was made in Germany and brought over to England many years ago. I always wear English clothes and I live in the attic of the very old English house. I enjoy every minute of my life here because I know all my friends love me, and Alice loves me too!

You can now see my face, eyes and my tiny little flat nose. My little thumb and finger are worn away, because many years ago a little girl to whom I belonged used to carry me by my left hand. Her hand was so small she had to hold me very tightly. After a few years my thumb and finger got worn away. They could be repaired but my owner says it would be wrong to give me a new thumb and finger, because losing my own is a great sign of the love the little girl had for me, she must have always carried me around with her.

I am now thinking of this afternoon, when Nanny is going to show me the fish in the pond. There are some enormous goldfish there and some very tiny fish. They have great fun swimming in and out of the water lilies which are growing all over the pond. In the middle of the pond, on a bed of water ferns, there is a bird's nest with three baby birds in it. I think they must be starlings. The young ones are very clever – they never attempt to get near the water.

Leonora

I am Leonora. I was discovered in the most adorable little antique toy shop in London. It has a bow fronted window with tiny panes of glass in. It was so nice being there. We would see toy collectors from all over the world coming into the shop. It was the sweetest little shop anyone could find anywhere, absolutely full of toys of all ages. Each time I was moved, I always ended up on the top shelf. That is why I was overlooked by most of the collectors.

I cannot tell you how happy I was to be brought to live in the attic here and not purchased by a dealer who would sell me again. The people here treat me as a very important little person. I had the first priority of choosing my pram, which is made by 'Dunkley'. It is so comfortable.

We have a special house for the prams because there isn't sufficient room in the attic to take all the prams, but this particular one is allocated to me. I am very proud of the fact.

Andrew

My name is Andrew and my greatest treat is to be allowed to watch the trains coming into the station. In this case do you not agree that 'Chin Chini' should also be with me. As a matter of fact, he isn't the slightest bit interested in the trains.

But back to Kowloon Station, it doesn't actually mean that we are in Hong Kong – we are still in England, but as you know, anything can happen when a little girl dreams.

We do have a fine collection of trains in the attic. Most of them are packed away in boxes – others are stationary.

The next train to arrive at Kowloon is the 3.30pm. After that it is time for me to return to the attic.

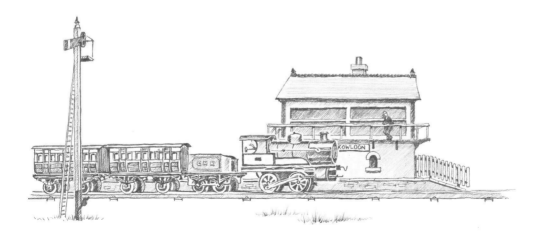

Richard

I have to meet Rebecca, Ruth and Rachel. I do hope they will wait for me. We arranged to meet at the Roseberry Rocks for afternoon tea.

It is really going to be a picnic, because Cook has been busy packing sandwiches, cakes and chocolate biscuits. That is why Nanny and I are late. We had to wait for Cook to finish the hamper, this means the other little dolls cannot eat until we arrive.
My name is Richard.

Patrick

I have been crying, not because I have been naughty, but simply because I have another tooth almost ready to come through. I already have two teeth. Nanny says I will be fine very soon. She has rubbed my gums with glycerine and honey. Now the pain has almost gone.

I will be able to eat jelly for tea. This is so refreshing and delicious, especially the lemon jelly.

My teething ring that I am holding is a tremendous help. It is rather beautiful, made of ivory, silver and pink coral. It is a Victorian one.

My name is Patrick.

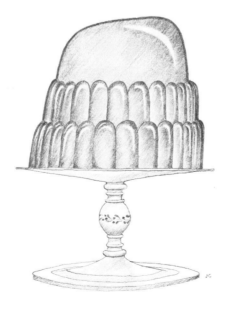

Charlie & Sam

What have we here? Oh no, oh yes! Another set of twins. Their names are Cheeky Charlie and Saucy Sam.

I wonder what mischief is brewing up in their little minds. First, I imagine the pram cover will come off, then the blanket. After that, the cushion will come flying out. Then I can see the twins will try and disembark from their carriage, but alas they cannot walk as yet, so there is no fear of them getting very far. Heaven knows what is in store for us, when they suddenly realise they can get up and walk.

On the whole they are very well behaved children, apart from attempting to pull each others hair and bite each others fingers.

They are going to hate returning from dreamland, but they will always retain their enchanting smiles, no matter what happens.

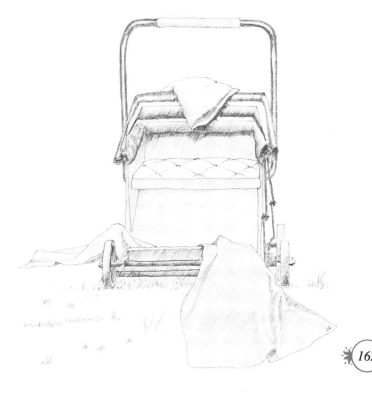

Jasmine

It is my Christening Day. My name is going to be 'Jasmine'. What a wonderful day it is going to be. The sun is shining, all the lady guests are looking so smart. They seem to be so full of admiration for me, and making very kind remarks about my dress.

The procedure is to take me to the magnificent little church in the next village. The village is called Mulberry. The church is literally four hundred years old. It has lovely highly coloured glass panelled windows, oak carved pews to sit in, and the romantic looking font where I will be christened, and where hundreds of little babies have been christened before.

Ruth

Can you see my dress? It is so beautiful. The skirt has four yards of material in it, with trimmings of fine Irish lace and a long length of pink ribbon threaded through.

I have so many petticoats underneath my dress to make it stand out. They are equally as attractive as the dress. I also have to wear a flannel petticoat – this has my initials on and a crest in the corner. I wish I could show it to you. This indicates I must have belonged to a family of great renown.

My name is Ruth and I am very happy here in my present surroundings. I do not ever wish to leave.

Ruby & Rachel

We are Ruby, Ruth and Rachel. We have had a wonderful day. Carmen came to meet us with her Nanny. They brought a picnic basket full of goodies that Cook had prepared.

Surprisingly, we have managed to remain clean. No marks of jam or tomatoes on our dresses.

We are so careful and take great care of our clothes, because they have been beautifully made with hand-stitching and hand-made laces. In fact, to preserve everything we are covered over with muslin sheets. It can get rather dusty in the attic.

Chapter
6

Goodbye

Babies of the Attic

We are called the Babies of the attic. We never cry, because we are dolls, and dolls do not cry. We are always smiling. Everyone adores us, especially real children. They love to be with us.

Although real children are not allowed in the attic, they do see us when we are brought down into the big room at Christmas time, which is so wonderful, because we are allowed to sit by the Christmas tree. Then all the little visitors are allowed to play with us, they do handle us with great care, our faces are made of china and could very easily break.

I almost forgot to tell you why we are sitting on the steps, the reason is to say "Goodbye". We do hope you have enjoyed meeting us, as we have appreciated your company as well.

In our prams we feel like little soldiers in a row. This is how we intend to return to the attic. We have so many happy memories of the garden, all the flowers, the little birds and animals.

"Goodbye!"

Magdeline and Matti are almost ready to return home. They have had a very happy and peaceful afternoon.

It takes quite a long time to get back to the attic. Matti's pram is rather hard-going, the wheels are made of cast iron and it is very difficult to push over the grass and gravel paths.

They say goodbye to the heather, all the beautiful flowers, everything they see in the garden to say goodbye to.

Like everyone Leonora has had a very exciting day. She went to the village. She found the village shop a fascinating place, displaying packets of food, cottons, tapes, candles, they seem to have just everything there.

Carmen and Katie are returning home, they have joined their little friend Karin who looks much bigger than she really is. Her Nanny put her in the high chair in the garden. She loves watching the trees, especially today when we have a slight breeze blowing the branches and leaves backwards and forwards.

She also enjoys seeing her friends strolling around, they all stop to talk to her. She loves the admiration she receives from them all.

Annabel feels unhappy to have to leave the garden. She saw the baby deer in the distance and the sheep with their baby lambs. She also saw the Highland cattle in the park, with their dear little calves looking like cuddly teddie bears with enormous eyes and very long eye-lashes.

She waved her "goodbyes" to all of them.

Knowing that Alice's dream must come to an end, Alexia realises that it is time to return to the attic.

She is going to meet up with Annabel, they will have a lot to discuss when they finally reach their destination.

Dear Dolly you are sleepy
It is time to go to bed
So on your little pillow
Lay down your tiny head
And Mummie will sing so softly
Sitting by your side
Till right away to slumberland
Dear Dolly you will glide.
Naughty Dolly you are peeping
Now close those eyelids tight
And listen to my slumber song
GOODNIGHT GOODNIGHT GOODNIGHT

(This is the Author's doll from childhood.)

Goodbye

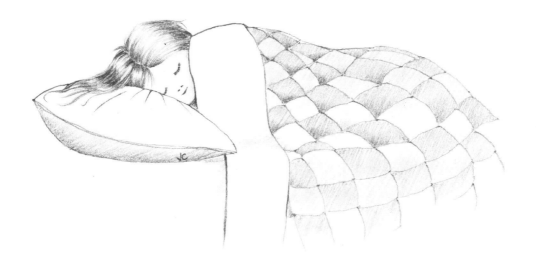

Appendix

Brief details are given below about each doll, its country of origin, maker and date of manufacture (where known) and size.

Name	Maker's Name	Year	Height	Page
ADAM	3 Face China Doll.	1920	12 ins	15
ALETHEA	Made in Germany by Armand Marseille.	1914	12 ins	141
ALEXIA	Made in Germany by C. M. Bergmann Walterhauser.	1916	18 ins	118/177
ALICIA	Made in Germany by P. M. Perzellan Fabrik Muchendorn.	1920	12 ins	121
ALICIA'S MUMMIE	Life-size model, double jointed including fingers. Wearing pure silk dress with hand-painted flowers.	1850 1875	60 ins	121
AMELIA	English Wax Doll.	1860	23 ins	15
ANDREW	This little doll is made of clay. It is very heavy and measures 7" high. No name or number.	1900		157
ANGELA	S.F.B.J. Paris No. 301. Pierced ears, bisque head.	1903	24 ins	27
ANITA	Made in Germany by Armand Marseille. No. 390 N.D.R.G.H. 246 A.I.I.	1905	16 ins	68
ANNA	German Wax Doll.	1875	25 ins	15
ANNABEL	Armand Marseille 390 Germany	1912	30 ins	126/177
ANNETTE	Bisque shoulder head, kid body, made by Armand Marseille, Germany.	1885	20 ins	55
ANORELLA	Leather body, composition head, made in America.	1875	20 ins	43
ANTHONY	Shop Model wearing blue velvet jacket and satin trousers	1815	49 ins	99

Name	Maker's Name	Year	Height	Page
BELINDA	"Rosebud" made by Horsman, Germany.	1920	18 ins	84
BETTY	Welsh dressed doll with kid body. Shoulder head bisque, also arms and legs. Made by Armand Marseille in Germany.	1895	16 ins	60
BRIDGET	Made in England by 'Deans Rag Book', Henry Samuel Dean. Reg. No. 890.903.	1918	36 ins	84
CAMILLE	Victorian Dress made by "Libertys" of London.	1920	33 ins	96
CARMEN	Made in Egypt. Wearing Victorian pink dress. A walking doll with moveable hands and legs. Composition head and body.	20th Century	36 ins	133/174
CAROLE	S.F.B.J. Paris	1903	18 ins	32
CARON	P.M. 23 Germany, Purzellanfabrik, Muchendorf.	1920	22 ins	24
CATALINA	Red silk dress with overlay of jet beads, embroidered on to black Honiton lace. Made by Platts Imperial House, Huddersfield.	1885	60 ins	112
CATHERINE	"Walkure" made by Klay and Hahn, Germany. Pierced ear, double jointed.	1902	24 ins	24
CECILIA	Made in Germany by Armand Marseille. No. 1894 A.M.D.E.P.	1870	12 ins	71/96
CHARLIE	Made by Reliable Toy Company, Toronto, Canada.	1924	20 ins	162
CHARLOTTE	Made by Heubach, Germany. No. 250 Koppelsdorf.	1890	14 ins	51
CHIN CHINI	Made in Germany by Armand Marseille. Closing eyes and bent body.	1920	12 ins	150/153

Name	Maker's Name	Year	Height	Page
CONSTANCE	Bisque shouldered head, arms and legs. White kid body. Made by Kestner, Germany, No. 3097.	1887	18 ins	80
	Baby doll made of celluloid in Germany.	1925		
CORAL	B.N.D. London. Mohair wig, composition head and body.	1920	15 ins	24
DOREEN	Made in Germany by Max Handwerk.	1912	25 ins	125
DOROTHY	Made in Germany by Simon and Halbig, for the firm of Cunno, Otto Dressel and Jurra.	1907	24 ins	125
DREAM DOLLY	Made by Armand Marseille, Germany 351/26.	1924	12 ins	178
EMMELINE	Pink, silk ball gown made by Deroy Schollicke, Dressmaker, Sheffield.	1885	60 ins	111
	Bag covered with beads and pearls.	1860.		
	Parasol - white silk with bone handle.	1845.		
FENNELLA	Ladies Boudoir Doll. Ref. no. 48061. V.V.E.5.D. and P.B.Patron 3462. Laceur 70. Made in France.	1885	36 ins	87
FRANCESCA	Ladies Boudoir Doll. Ref. no. 48061. V.V.E.5.D. and P. B. Patron 3462. Laceur 70. Made in France.	1885	30 ins	87
FRANCOISE	S.F.B.J. Paris No. 60.	1903	10 ins	28
GEORGE	Character Doll made in Germany by J. D. Kestner.	1896	12 ins	149
GRANDMA	Small House Doll.	1870	5 ins	20
HANNAH	Kid body, bisque shoulder head, composition hands and legs. Made by Cund and Otto Dressell, Germany.	1890	15 ins	63

Name	Maker's Name	Year	Height	Page
HARRIET	Bisque shoulder head with closed mouth, dimple. No. 3097. Made by Kestner, Germany.	1887	18 ins	63
HETTY	House Doll made in Germany. Note on base "Please Mam which room shall I sweep next?"	1840	6 ins	59
JACQUELINE	S.F.B.J. Paris. No. 60.	1903	10 ins	28
JANEY	Simon and Halbig. Composition ball jointed body. China head, pierced ears, open mouth. Made in Germany.	1900	17 ins	31
JASMINE	Made by Armand Marseille, Germany. No. 990 A.10.M.	1910	20 ins	165
JEMIMA	Frozen Charlotte Doll.	1890	4 ins	23
JEREMY	Ivory cream satin suit, white kid gloves. Lace on suit and Jabot Argentinian lace. 18th century suit.	1810	62 ins	100
JOANNA	Wax face, body stuffed with hair. English made.	1865	18 ins	16
JOSEPH	Sailor suit made by Brights, Bournemouth. "Sailors Rowe".	1920	33 ins	96
JOSEPHINE	Wax face, stuffed body. English made.	1865	16 ins	16
KARIN	Made by Heubach No. 320, Koppelsdorf, Germany. Karin is wearing a Victorian Christening Gown.	1909	20 ins	174
KAROLINA	French doll made by S.F.B.J., Societé Francaise de Fabrication de Bébés et Jouets. It has pierced ears, china face. No. 60.	1903	18 ins	23

Name	Maker's Name	Year	Height	Page
KATIE	Details as Carmen. The dress and bonnet were made by De Stitsche Nyvermeid Utrecht, Holland.	1890	36 ins	133/174
LEONORA	Made in Germany by Armand Marseille	1914	20 ins	154/173
LETITIA	Shop model wearing mauve silk moire dress with pure silk sash, hand painted flowers, bag to match. Made by Jeanne Hallee, Rueville, Leveque, Paris.	1870	60 ins	103/107/108
	Shoes cream satin embroidered with art diamonds, rubies and pearls.	1850		
LINDA	Morimura Bros, New York.	1920	18 ins	83
LINDY	Small House doll. Made in France.	1875	5 ins	20
LORETTA	China head, stuffed body.	1875	8 ins	134
LORNA	Parian head, arms and legs. Hard stuffed body.	1870	8 ins	134
LUCINDA	Small House doll, made in France.	1875	5 ins	20
LUCY	Small House doll, made in France.	1875	4 ins	20
MABEL	Kid body with bisque head, arms and legs. Made by Armand Marseille in Germany.	1905	24 ins	56
MAGDELINE	Made in Germany by C. Bergmann.	1910	20 ins	137/173
MANDY	Made in Germany by Armand Marseille.	1910	20 ins	142
MARGARETTE	Made in Germany by Armand Marseille. No. A&M2.O.X.D.E.P.	1894	18 ins	48
MARIA	Made by Mayer and Sherratt, England. Marked Melba.	1915	17 ins	48
MARTHA	Schoenan and Huffmeister, Bavaria, Germany. No. 5.	1909	20 ins	12

Name	Maker's Name	Year	Height	Page
MARY	Made in Japan by "Murimura".	1920	18 ins	145/146
MATTI	Made in Germany by Armand Marseille.	1895	12 ins	138/173
MILDRED	Hermann Steiner	1921	22 ins	12
MONIQUE	S.F.B.J. Paris No. 60.	1903	10 ins	28
OLIVIA	Papier maché head covered with wax, cotton stuffed body, composition hands and legs. No maker's name.	1885	26 ins	130
PAMELA	Made by Armand Marseille in Germany. Bisque head, arms and legs. No. 995 A.i0.M.	1914	18 ins	83
PATRICIA	Made by Simon and Halbig, Germany.	1910	29 ins	122
PATRICK	Made in Germany by Armand Marseille.	1924	18 ins	161
PAULINE	Made in Germany by Simon and Halbig. This doll has manually moving eyelids.	1905	29 ins	122
PAVLA	Papier maché head with double jointed body. No name, possibly made by Novelty Co., America.	1915	25 ins	51
PETRA	Made in Germany by Simon and Halbig.	1909	29 ins	122
PETULA	Shop model wearing dress made by Mrs. Rhind of Sussex Place, London.	1885	37 ins	96
PHOEBE	Blue dress, bisque head. Made by Ernst Heubach No. 250-4, Germany.	1900	24 ins	40
PRISCILLA	Wax face, clear glass eyes. Made in France.	1865	18 ins	19
PRUDENCE	Made by Simon and Halbig in Germany.	1909	24 ins	56
PRUNELLA	Simon and Halbig, merged with Kammer and Rainhardt, Germany.	1910	18 ins	35/36

Name	Maker's Name	Year	Height	Page
RACHEL	Made in Germany by Armand Marseille. No. 351.	1920	18 ins	166
REBECCA	Made by Simon and Halbig No. 55.	1903	21 ins	39/83
RICHARD	Made by Reliable Toy Company, Toronto, Canada.	1922	10 ins	158
ROSE	Pink afternoon dress with embroidered bag, made by Kirby and Nicholson, Manchester.	1870	60 ins	104/107/108
RUBY	Made by Armand Marseille, Germany.	1920	14 ins	166
RUTH	J.D.K. made by Kestner, Germany.	1920	14 ins	166
SAM	Made by Reliable Toy Company, Toronto, Canada.	1924	20 ins	162
SARAH	Poured wax over papier maché head, cream kid body.	1860	20 ins	32
SOPHIA	Parian Bisque type made by John Ridgeway, England.	1865	15 ins	67
SUZIE	Kestner. Bisque head and hands. Kid body.	1910	14 ins	31
TESSA	Composition face, arms and legs. Stuffed body. Animal skin, hair. Made in Germany.	1910	15 ins	75
TINY	Composition face, arms and legs. Stuffed body, animal skin, hair. Made in Germany.	1910	14 ins	75
TOBY	Papier maché head, composition body. Made in France.	1929	26 ins	52
URITA	Made by Rosebud.	1920	18 ins	72
VALERIE	Made by Armand Marseille, Germany.	1905	36 ins	129

Name	Maker's Name	Year	Height	Page
VICTORIA	Black velvet and satin ribbon dress made by Mme. L. Storch, Paris. Also makers of elegant beaded capes.	1880	60 ins	115
	Handbag - black velvet with steel embossed frame.	1850		
VIRGINIA	Made in Germany by Kestner	1900	20 ins	44
WENDY	Bisque head, made in Germany by Armand Marseille.	1895	20 ins	64
WILHELMINA	White fine lawn heavily embroidered dress with cream woollen cloak.	1850	54 ins	100

N.B. Dates quoted for shop models refer to garments.

The author—Meggi Bamford